It's about Time

Seconds

by Kimberly M. Hutmacher

Gail Saunders-Smith, PhD,
Consulting Editor

CAPSTONE PRESS
a capstone imprint

Pebble Books are published by Capstone Press,
1710 Roe Crest Drive, North Mankato, Minnesota 56003
www.capstonepub.com

Library of Congress Cataloging-in-Publication Data
Hutmacher, Kimberly.
  Seconds / by Kimberly M. Hutmacher.
    p. cm.—(Pebble Books. It's about time)
  Includes bibliographical references and index.
  Summary: "Simple rhyming text and color photographs present seconds as a unit
of time"—Provided by publisher.
  ISBN 978-1-4296-8575-7 (library binding)
  ISBN 978-1-4296-9354-7 (pbk.)
  ISBN 978-1-62065-285-5 (ebook PDF)
  1. Time—Juvenile literature. 2. Time measurements—Juvenile literature. 3. Clocks
and watches—Juvenile literature. I. Title.
  QB209.5.H886 2013
  529'.2—dc23   2012004670

Note to Parents and Teachers

The It's about Time set supports national mathematics standards
related to measurement and data. This book describes and
illustrates seconds. The images support early readers in
understanding the text. The repetition of words and phrases helps
early readers learn new words. This book also introduces early
readers to subject-specific vocabulary words, which are defined
in the Glossary section. Early readers may need assistance to read
some words and to use the Table of Contents, Glossary, Read More,
Internet Sites, and Index sections of the book.

Printed in the United States of America in North Mankato, Minnesota.

042012   006682CGF12

Table of Contents

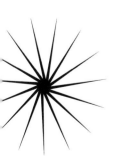

What Is a Second?

A second is

a bit of time.

Let's learn seconds

with this rhyme.

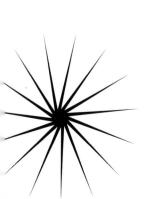

6

Telling Time with Seconds

Clocks help us

measure time,

count our seconds,

coo and chime.

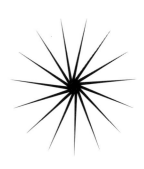

minute hand

a second

hour hand

second hand

There are three hands
that circle clocks.
The second's fastest.
The second rocks!

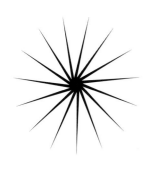

The second hand
rounds the face—
60 seconds
back to place.

How Long Is a Second?

A second passes by you when ...

You clap your hands.

Stomp your feet.

Snap your fingers.

Drum a beat.

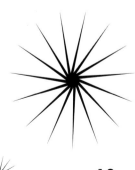

Turn your head.

Sneeze, "Achoo!"

Kick a ball.

Tap a shoe.

Jump a rope.

Swing a bat.

Switch a channel.

Pet a cat.

Do a push-up.

Turn a page.

Pop a bubble.

Bow on stage!

These are seconds
ticking by.
Gone in one wink
of an eye!

Glossary

chime—a ringing sound

clock—something used to measure and show time

coo—a low, soft sound like that made by a dove or pigeon

face—the front side of a clock; it shows the numbers and hands of the clock

hand—a pointer on a clock

second—a unit of time that is one of 60 equal parts of a minute

stage—a flat, raised area on which people perform

Read More

Jenkins, Steve. *Just a Second.* Boston: Houghton Mifflin Books for Children, 2011.

Murphy, Patricia J. *Telling Time with Puppies and Kittens.* Puppy and Kitten Math. Berkeley Heights, N.J.: Enslow Publishers, 2007.

Steffora, Tracey. *What Is Time?* Chicago: Heinemann Library, 2012.

Internet Sites

FactHound offers a safe, fun way to find Internet sites related to this book. All of the sites on FactHound have been researched by our staff.

Here's all you do:

Visit *www.facthound.com*

Type in this code: 9781429685757

Index

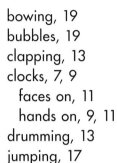

Word Count: 115
Grade: 1
Early-Intervention Level: 14

Editorial Credits
Gillia Olson, editor; Lori Bye, designer; Sarah Schuette, photo stylist;
    Marcy Morin, studio scheduler; Kathy McColley, production specialist

Photo Credits
All photos by Capstone Studio/Karon Dubke except:
    Shutterstock/Mark Herreid, cover (back)